RUBY the COPYCAT

by
Peggy Rathmann

SCHOLASTIC
HARDCOVER

SCHOLASTIC INC.
New York

The artwork in this book was prepared with colored pencil and ink.

Copyright © 1991 by Margaret Rathmann

All rights reserved. Published by Scholastic Inc.

Scholastic Hardcover is a registered trademark of Scholastic Inc.

Library of Congress Cataloging-in-Publication Data
Rathmann, Peggy.
Ruby the Copycat/by Peggy Rathmann.
p. cm.
Summary: Ruby insists on copying Angela, until her teacher helps
her discover her own creative resources.
ISBN 0-590-43747-X
[1. Behavior–Fiction. 2. Teacher-student relationships–Fiction.
3. Schools–Fiction.] I. Title.
PZ7.R1936Ru 1991   91-101
[E]–dc20   CIP
AC

12 11 10 9 8 7 6 5 4 3 2 1   1 2 3 4 5 6/9

Printed in the U.S.A.   36

First Scholastic printing, November 1991

Designed by Tracy Arnold

*For Grammy Joy and Papa George,
who always try to set a good example.*

*Special thanks to Loma Vista School and
Pierpont School of Ventura.*

Monday was Ruby's first day in Miss Hart's class.

"Class, this is Ruby," announced Miss Hart.
"Ruby, you may use the empty desk behind Angela.
Angela is the girl with the pretty red bow in her hair."

Angela smiled at Ruby.

Ruby smiled at Angela's bow and tiptoed
to her seat.

"I hope everyone had a pleasant weekend," said
Miss Hart. "Does anyone have something to share?"

"I was the flower girl at my sister's wedding,"
said Angela.

"That's exciting," said Miss Hart.

Ruby raised her hand halfway. "I was the flower girl at my sister's wedding, too."

"What a coincidence!" said Miss Hart.

Angela turned and smiled at Ruby.

Ruby smiled at the top of Angela's head.

"Class, please take out your reading books," said Miss Hart.

At lunchtime, Ruby hopped all the way home on one foot.

When Ruby came back to school,
she was wearing a red bow in her hair.
She slid into her seat behind Angela.

"I like your bow," whispered Angela.

"I like yours, too," whispered Ruby.

"Class, please take out your math books,"
said Miss Hart.

On Tuesday morning,
Angela wore a sweater with
daisies on it.

At lunchtime, Ruby
hopped home sideways.

When Ruby came back to school after lunch,
she was wearing a sweater with daisies on it.
"I like your sweater," whispered Angela.
"I like yours, too," whispered Ruby.

On Wednesday, Angela wore a hand-painted
T-shirt with matching sneakers.

After lunch, Ruby hopped back to school wearing
a hand-painted T-shirt with matching sneakers.

"Why are you sitting like that?" whispered Angela.

"Wet paint," said Ruby.

On Thursday morning, during Sharing Time,
Angela modeled the flower girl dress
she wore at her sister's wedding.

Ruby modeled her flower girl dress, too,
right after lunch.

Angela didn't whisper anything.

By coincidence, on Friday morning, both girls wore red-and-lavender-striped dresses.

At lunchtime, Angela raced home.

When Angela came back to school,
she was wearing black.

On Friday afternoon, Miss Hart asked everyone to write a short poem.

"Who would like to read first?" asked Miss Hart.

Angela raised her hand. She stood by her desk and read:

I had a cat I could not see,
Because it stayed in back of me.
It was a very loyal pet—
It's sad we never really met.

"That was very good!" said Miss Hart. "Now, who's next?" Miss Hart looked around the room. "Ruby?"

Ruby stood and recited slowly:

I had a nice pet,
Who I never met,
Because it always stayed behind me.
And I'm sure it was a cat, too.

Ruby smiled at the back of Angela's head.
Someone whispered. Ruby sat down.
"What a coincidence," murmured Miss Hart.

Angela scribbled something on a piece of paper. She passed it to Ruby.

The note said:

YOU COPIED ME!
I'M TELLING MISS HART!
P.S. I HATE YOUR HAIR THAT WAY.

Ruby buried her chin in the collar of her blouse. A big tear rolled down her nose and plopped onto the note.

When the bell rang, Miss Hart sent everyone home except Ruby.

Miss Hart closed the door of the schoolroom
and sat on the edge of Ruby's desk.

"Ruby, dear," she said gently, "you don't need to
copy everything Angela does. You can be anything
you want to be, but be Ruby first. I like Ruby."

Miss Hart smiled at Ruby. Ruby smiled at
Miss Hart's beautiful, polished fingernails.
"Have a nice weekend," said Miss Hart.
"Have a nice weekend," said Ruby.

On Monday morning, Miss Hart said, "I hope everyone had a pleasant weekend. I did! I went to the opera." Miss Hart looked around the room. "Does anyone have something to share?"

Ruby waved her hand. Glued to every finger was a pink plastic fingernail.

"I went to the opera, too!" said Ruby.

"She did not!" whispered Angela.

Miss Hart folded her hands
and looked very serious.
"Ruby, dear," said Miss Hart
gently, "did you do anything else
this weekend?"

Ruby peeled off a fingernail.

"I hopped," said Ruby.

The class giggled.

Ruby's ears turned red.

"But I did! I hopped around the picnic table ten times!" Ruby looked around the room. "Watch!"

Ruby sprang from her desk.

She hopped forward.

She hopped backward.

She hopped sideways with both eyes shut.

The class cheered and clapped their hands
to the beat of Ruby's feet. Ruby was the best
hopper they had ever seen.

Miss Hart turned on the tape player and said,
"Follow the leader! Do the Ruby Hop!"
So Ruby led the class around the room,
while everyone copied *her*.

And at noon, Ruby and Angela hopped home for lunch.